Sammy ♡

from Erin

THE BUTTER TREE

· Tales of Bruh Rabbit ·

T·H·E
BUTTER TREE

· Tales of Bruh Rabbit ·

Retold by

MARY E. LYONS

Illustrated by

MIREILLE VAUTIER

Henry Holt and Company
New York

Henry Holt and Company, Inc.
Publishers since 1866
115 West 18th Street
New York, New York 10011

Henry Holt is a registered
trademark of Henry Holt and Company, Inc.

Published in Canada by Fitzhenry & Whiteside Ltd.,
195 Allstate Parkway, Markham, Ontario L3R 4T8.

Library of Congress Cataloging-in-Publication Data
Lyons, Mary (Mary E.)
The butter tree; tales of Bruh Rabbit / retold by Mary E. Lyons;
illustrated by Mireille Vautier.
Contents: Bruh Bear plays dead—Bruh Bear's fish—The butter
tree—Bruh Rabbit fools Bruh Wolf—Bruh Wolf fools Bruh Rabbit—
Bruh Rabbit and Bruh Guinea Fowl—The stories.
1. Afro-Americans—South Carolina—Folklore. 2. Folklore—South
Carolina. [1. Afro-Americans—Folklore. 2. Folklore—South
Carolina. 3. Animals—Folklore.] I. Vautier, Mireille, ill. II. Title.
PZ8.1.L986Bu 1995 [398.24'52'09757]—dc20 94-8407

ISBN 0-8050-2673-8

First Edition—1995

Printed in the United States of America
on acid-free paper. ∞

1 3 5 7 9 10 8 6 4 2

Contents

Foreword

The animals in Bruh Rabbit tales remind us of ourselves. They eat, play, work, and sleep just as we do. Sometimes they help each other. But sometimes they play tricks.

THE BUTTER TREE
· Tales of Bruh Rabbit ·

Bruh Bear Plays Dead

Bruh Bear and Bruh Rabbit liked to chase each other. One day Bruh Rabbit found Bruh Bear at his house. All the animals were there. But Bruh Bear was in bed and under the sheet. He was not breathing.

Bruh Rabbit squinched down in the door. He said, "My, my, so Bear is dead."

"Yes, poor Bear!" the animals said.

Bruh Rabbit did not believe it. He made a plan.

He called out, "They say if a bear is dead, he turns over. Then he groans three times." Big old Bear turned over. He groaned three times.

"Ha, ha!" Bruh Rabbit said. "A dead bear can't groan like that." Then Bruh Rabbit laughed again and jumped outside.

Bruh Bear was right behind him, sheet and all. But there was nothing to *that* race. Bruh Bear is big. But he can't ever outrun Bruh Rabbit!

Bruh Bear's Fish

One time Bruh Bear caught a nice mess of fish. Bruh Rabbit got hungry seeing the fat fish. He ran through the woods ahead of Bruh Bear. Then he lay down in the path and closed his eyes.

Bruh Bear came along. "My, my, that is a pity. There is a sick Bruh Rabbit." And he went on down the path.

Bruh Rabbit jumped up. He cut through the woods again. Then he fell down in the path.

When Bruh Bear saw him, he said, "My,

my, that is a pity. Here is another poor Bruh Rabbit.''

Bruh Bear kept on down the path. The next time he saw a rabbit, he laid down his fish. ''I think I will go back and get all the other ones,'' he said.

Bruh Bear walked, walked, walked, but there were no rabbits on the path. Then he went back for his catch. He did not find his fish

either. But he saw Bruh Rabbit with a big iron pot. Turnip greens and collard greens were floating on top.

"Hey!" said Bruh Bear. "I smell fish cooking."

"Oh, no," Bruh Rabbit told him. "Only collards and turnips with plenty of bacon. See?" Bruh Rabbit stirred the pot with an old cook spoon.

"My nose can't fool me!" said Bruh Bear. He took the spoon. And he turned up all the fish from the bottom of the pot.

Then Bruh Rabbit said, "Well, I got big business down the road." He ran faster than a straight line. Bruh Bear chased him right through the woods. But Bruh Bear never catches Bruh Rabbit. No, sir!

The Butter Tree

Bruh Rabbit and Bruh Wolf had a butter tree next to a rice field. One day they went to hoe the rice. Rabbit was hungry and said, "I am going home now. My wife is calling."

Rabbit slipped through the bushes to the tree and ate some butter. He came back and picked up his hoe. He told Wolf, "My wife has a young one at home. She wanted me to give it a name."

Wolf said, "What did you name it?"

"JUST STARTED," Rabbit told him.

They hoed the rice. Soon Rabbit was ready to eat again. "My wife is calling," he said. "I have more children to name." He slipped to the butter tree and filled up. He came back.

Wolf asked, "What did you name the child?"

"ALMOST HALF," Rabbit said.

Rabbit hoed and hoed. He thought about the butter tree. That made him hungry again. "Bruh Wolf, my wife calls," he said. "She must want me to name another child." He slipped through the bushes and filled up at the butter tree.

When he came back, Wolf asked, "What did you name it?"

"ALMOST GONE!"

Rabbit hoed again. Just before lunch he felt hungry. He threw down his hoe and said, "Bruh Wolf, I have to name that last child." He left so fast that he almost lost his wind.

When Rabbit came back, Wolf asked, "What did you name the last one?"

"ALL GONE!"

Rabbit hoed until Wolf called, "NOON! Time to eat our butter."

All the butter was gone when they got to the tree. But Bruh Rabbit was sharp. He acted mad. He said, "Bruh Wolf, you ate all the butter."

Wolf told him, "No! Not me!"

Rabbit said, "Tell you what. We will lie down and rest. The sun will shine hot. We can tell who ate the butter. It will melt and run out of his mouth."

The sun was warm. Wolf was tired. He lay down and went to sleep. Rabbit took butter from his mouth and put it on Wolf's lips.

When Wolf woke up, Rabbit said, "Bruh Wolf, you ate the butter. It is all over your mouth!" Then Wolf ran home as fast as he could.

Bruh Rabbit rubbed his belly. He was already thinking about supper.

Bruh Rabbit Fools Bruh Wolf

Once upon a time, Bruh Rabbit and Bruh Wolf went fishing. They both got wet. Bruh Rabbit said, "Come home with me, Bruh Wolf."

Bruh Rabbit climbed in his bake oven and came out dry.

"Now, Bruh Wolf," he said, "you get in the oven. Knock when you are dry!"

Bruh Wolf got in the oven. KNOCK! KNOCK!

Bruh Rabbit said, "Old man, you are not

dry yet." Bruh Wolf knocked again. "No, sir,"
said Bruh Rabbit. "Still not dry!"

Bruh Wolf knocked one more time. Bruh
Rabbit opened the oven door a crack. He
peeked inside. "Chin-chin," he said. "I want
you crispy dry."

Then he slammed the door. And Bruh
Rabbit's children had oven-fried wolf for
supper.

Bruh Wolf Fools Bruh Rabbit

ꭶꮢꮄꮢ

Bruh Wolf fooled Bruh Rabbit this time. Bruh Wolf had a good bunch of fish. On the way home he met Bruh Rabbit. Bruh Rabbit said, "Hello! How did you get the fish?"

"You can catch all the fish you want," Bruh Wolf told him. "Just do like I do. Go down to the creek. Sit on a log and drop your tail in the water. Shake it around and bob it up and down. When a fish bites your tail, pull him up.

Then string him on your line. Keep that up until your string is full."

Bruh Rabbit did what Bruh Wolf said. He sat on a log and dropped his tail in the water. But the black frost came. It was so cold that Bruh Rabbit could only wiggle the tip of his tail.

Soon the water froze. Bruh Rabbit decided to leave. He tried to get up. But he could not pull his tail out of the ice.

Bruh Coo-Coo Owl was up in the tree. Bruh Rabbit yelled, "Hey! Come here, Bruh Owl! A fish has got my tail."

Bruh Owl flew down to help Bruh Rabbit. He grabbed him by both ears. He pulled as hard as he could. Bruh Rabbit's ears began to stretch. His eyes popped out.

Then Bruh Owl grabbed Bruh Rabbit's tail. He pulled him out of the black frost. But the tail came right off! To this day, Bruh Rabbit has long ears, big eyes, and no tail. No fish, either.

Bruh Rabbit and Bruh Guinea Fowl

One day Bruh Rabbit and Bruh Guinea saw a cow. Bruh Rabbit pointed to the sun. "Bruh Guinea," he said. "Do you see the red fire over there? Go get a piece of that fire. We will cook the cow."

Bruh Guinea flew day and night. But the sun was too far away. When he came back, he saw Bruh Rabbit but no cow. Only the tail, lying on the ground. Bruh Rabbit had given all the meat to his kin.

"Where is the cow?" asked Bruh Guinea.

"In the wink of an eye, the cow sunk into the ground," Bruh Rabbit said. "Nothing is left but the tail. If we pull the tail, we will find the cow."

They pulled. The tail came off the ground. Bruh Rabbit said, "Let's dig." They dug until they came to water. But still they did not find the cow.

Bruh Guinea said, "I am hungry. I will roast the tail and eat it." But when he ate the tail, he fell down and played dead.

Bruh Rabbit said, "Uh-oh. That meat is poisoned!" He ran to his family and brought back all the meat.

Bruh Guinea sat up and said, "You cannot fool me! We are going to split this food!" So Bruh Rabbit took his share. Bruh Guinea took his share. They left for home.

Then the man who owned the cow saw them. They threw the meat in the bushes and ran. When the man was gone, they raced back for the meat. But who got there first?

Step on a tin.
The tin bends.
That is the way
My story ends!

The Stories

When Africans arrived in America, they brought their memories with them. They remembered how to fix food in an African way, how to make music with an African sound, and how to tell African tales.

The enslaved people continued to tell stories about African animals like rabbit, owl, and guinea fowl. The animals that they found in America, such as bear and wolf, became part of the stories too.

Animal tales made the slaves laugh. Hearing

how small animals could trick big ones (and be tricked in return!) helped them live through slavery. Many of their tales were about finding food. So the stories also reminded slaves of ways to survive hungry times.

"Bruh" is a short way to say "brother." The animals in the stories also call each other "Buh," "Bruddah," or "Brer." "Bruh Rabbit Fools Bruh Wolf" is from Beaufort County, South Carolina. The other stories are from Murrells Inlet, South Carolina. They were all collected between 1935 and 1941 and first published in *South Carolina Folk Tales: Stories of Animals and Supernatural Beings*.

The tales are retold here so that readers of all ages can enjoy what the people called "All de bes' story."